First published in Great Britain 2000
by Mammoth
an imprint of Egmont Children's Books Limited
239 Kensington High Street, London W8 6SA
10 9 8 7 6 5 4 3 2 1

Text by Elizabeth Laird copyright ©
Egmont Children's Books Limited 2000
Illustrations copyright © Simone Lia 2000
ISBN 0 7497 3576 7

A CIP catalogue record for this title is available from the British Library

Printed in Hong Kong

The Great Big Enormous Turnip

Once upon a time, there was an old man who planted some turnip seeds in his garden. He watered them and weeded them and soon they began to grow.

Some of the seeds produced tiny leaves. Some of them produced ordinary-sized leaves, but one seed produced great big enormous leaves, and under the ground a great big enormous turnip began to grow.

The old man watched it and weeded it and watered it. It was the biggest turnip he had ever seen.

The day came when the turnip was ready to be pulled up. The old man grasped the leaves and he began to pull.

He pulled and pulled, but the turnip wouldn't move at all.

"Wife! Wife!" called the old man. "Come and help me pull up my great big turnip!"

So the old man's wife came running, and she held him around the waist, and she pulled the old man, and he pulled the turnip, but the turnip wouldn't move at all.

"Daughter, daughter!" called the old woman. "Come and help us pull up this great big turnip!"

So the old woman's daughter came running, and she took hold of the old woman's apron, and the girl pulled the old woman, and the old woman pulled the old man, and the old man pulled the turnip, but the turnip wouldn't move at all.

"Dog, dog!" called the daughter. "Come and help us pull up this great big turnip!"

So the dog came running up, and he took hold of the girl's skirt, and the dog pulled the girl, and the girl pulled the old woman, and the old woman pulled the old man, and the old man pulled the turnip, but still the turnip wouldn't move at all.

"Cat, cat!" called the dog. "Come and help us pull up this great big turnip!"

So the cat came running, and she took hold of the dog's tail, and the cat pulled the dog, and the dog pulled the girl, and the girl pulled the old woman, and the old woman pulled the old man, and the old man pulled the turnip, but even now the turnip wouldn't move at all.

"Mouse, mouse!" called the cat. "Come and help us pull up this great big turnip!"

So the mouse came running, and he took hold of the cat's tail, and the mouse pulled the cat, and the cat pulled the dog, and the dog pulled the girl, and the girl pulled the old woman, and the old woman pulled the old man, and the old man pulled the turnip, but still the turnip wouldn't move at all.

"Pull harder, just one more time," the old man shouted, and everyone pulled, and pulled and PULLED and the turnip shot out of the ground so fast that they all fell over in a great big heap.

"Will you look at that now," the old man said. "It's the biggest turnip that ever grew."

That night, the old woman made delicious turnip soup, and there was enough for everyone that day and the day after and the day after that.

The Magic Porridge Pot

Once there was a little girl who lived with her mother in a cottage by the woods. They were very poor, and the day came when they had nothing left to eat.

"I'll go into the woods to look for wild berries," the little girl said, and she took her basket and set off at once.

Soon she met an old woman.

"Where are you going, little girl?" the old woman said.

"To look for wild berries," said the little girl, "because my mother and I have nothing left to eat.

"You're a good girl," the old woman said, "and you don't need to look for berries any more. Take this pot to your mother and you will never be hungry again. When you get home, put it on the stove and say, 'Cook, little pot, cook!' It will fill up at once with porridge. And when you have eaten all that you want, just say, 'Stop, little pot, stop!' and it will stop making porridge until you ask it to make some more."

The little girl ran home to her mother as fast as her legs could carry her, and at once they put the little pot on the stove.

"Cook, little pot, cook!" said the little girl, and immediately delicious hot porridge bubbled up from the bottom of the pot. The little girl and her mother filled their plates and ate and ate until they could eat no more.

"Stop, little pot, stop!" said the little girl at last, and at once the pot stopped making porridge.

From that day on, the little girl and the mother lived very happily, for they always had plenty of porridge.

But one day, when the little girl had gone out to play, her mother was hungry. She fetched the pot down from its shelf and set it on the stove.

"Cook, little pot, cook!" she said, and at once the porridge pot was full.

The woman ate and ate until she could eat no more.

"I must stop the pot making any more porridge," she said to herself, but she couldn't remember what to say.

"Enough, little pot, enough," she said, but the porridge kept on bubbling up. It filled the pot to the brim and began to spill over the edge onto the stove.

"No more, little pot, no more!" the woman cried, but the porridge was coming out of the pot faster and faster. It was running off the stove and onto the floor. It was filling up the kitchen!

"Wait, little pot, wait!" shouted the woman, but the porridge was flowing out of the kitchen and into the lane.

"Help! What can I do? Oh, help!" the poor woman screamed, but still the porridge kept coming, flowing on and on in a delicious sticky stream, filling up the lane, running into the neighbours' gardens, pouring into every house in the village.

"What's this?" mewed the cats, sniffing at the porridge with their silky black noses.

"What's going on?" barked the dogs, licking at the porridge with their long red tongues and flicking it away with their hairy tails.

And all the while the little girl's mother was running up and down, trying to remember the magic words.

"Halt, little pot, halt!" she shouted, but the porridge kept on flowing.

Just as the porridge reached the last house in the village, the little girl came home. When she saw the porridge filling up the houses and flowing down the lane, and her mother running up and down, she called out, "Stop, little pot, stop!"

The porridge pot stopped at once, and everyone breathed a sigh of relief. They settled down to eating it all up, the men and women, the boys and girls, the cats and the dogs, but they had to swallow a lot of porridge before they could eat their way home.